HOW THE WEST WAS LOST IN A POKER GAME

SHORT STORIES AND POEMS

BY
KEN MILLER

ISBN: 978-1-64184-985-2 (paperback)
ISBN: 978-1-64184-984-5 (ebook)

This book is dedicated to my great niece,
Johonah, and great nephew, Simon.
It was originally written for their enjoyment.
It is because of them it is now available
to everyone!

The following short stories are works of fiction.
They are not meant to be historically accurate
but are comedies intended to brighten your day!

Enjoy!

TABLE OF CONTENTS

HOW THE WEST WAS LOST IN A POKER GAME

CHAPTER 1

Good morning. I am Max Seagle, and my story starts in Boston, Massachusetts, in 1865. My father had died of cancer a few months earlier, and my mother died during childbirth. I was a 24-year-old graduate of Harvard University and out to make my fortune. I was booked on the 9:15 a.m. train to Chicago, where my Uncle Bob Miller lived. He had offered me a job on his ranch.

I boarded a train on the Union Pacific Railroad. The conductor helped me find my seat and hollered, "All Aboard!" The train started with a jerk and soon began the clickety-clack sound that would keep me company for the next two days.

It was about noon on the first day when I started feeling hungry. I met the most beautiful gal on my way to the dining car. Her name was Susan Jones. (I knew I was in love at first sight and hoped to someday make her my wife!) The steward seated us together. We ordered food, and I told her about my new job opportunity. She was thrilled. She was returning home after a visit to Boston, where she had visited her relatives and done some sightseeing. She ran a flower shop in downtown Chicago. We had a lovely lunch of Steak, French Fries, and Coffee. We made plans to eat dinner together that night.

At one of the train stops, a well-dressed gentleman got on and sat beside me. His name was Joe Smith, and he was a gambler. I asked him if he could teach me poker and blackjack. He said he would be happy to. I picked them up quickly, and Joe said I was a natural! He recommended I become a professional gambler.

Sue and I met for dinner that night. We had the pork chop dinner with all the trimmings. We had a good time, and Sue kissed me on the way back to our seats.

I finally arrived in Chicago. My Uncle Bob Miller was waiting for me.

"Welcome to Chicago! Let me take your bag. Let's go have a beer," he said.

"Okay," I said.

Uncle Bob said, "I have a large ranch a few miles out of town, and you'll stay with me there."

My uncle and I got on the wagon and rode off to his ranch, which he called Miller Manor. It spread out over 200 acres. Uncle Bob introduced me to the ranch hands as his nephew and his new foreman.

That night Uncle Bob had a big Bar-B-Q. I had a juicy cheeseburger and a Pepsi-Cola. We went into the house for a talk when the party was over.

Uncle Bob said, "Max, you are home! If you don't like ranch work, I have a friend who owns the Armour meat packing house who said he would hire you. The problem with the meat packing house is there is a lot of blood in that job."

The next day we started branding cattle. It took all day, but we finished at about 6:00 p.m. I cleaned up and went into town for the barn dance, where I ran into Susan Jones. We danced the night away. As we left the barn, I leaned in and kissed her. We said goodnight and went our ways.

The next morning, Uncle Bob said, "Let's go fishing."

"Okay by me," I said.

We went fishing in Lake Michigan, where I caught two largemouth bass, and Uncle Bob caught three trout and one largemouth bass. We had a great day!

The next morning, Uncle Bob rode into town, leaving me at the ranch to fix some sections of broken fence. I had the whole crew on the project. At noon I rode back to the house to get sandwiches and lemonade for the crew. I entered the house and found Jack Fields, the old foreman, breaking into Uncle Bob's safe and cleaning out all the money.

I yelled, "What are you doing?"

He jumped me, and we started fighting. I grabbed one of Uncle Bob's guns and shot him. I got the food and took it to the crew. Uncle Bob returned to the ranch, and I told him what had happened. Uncle Bob told one of his men to take the body into town to the sheriff and tell him what had happened. Uncle Bob told me the sheriff might come to the ranch to investigate.

The sheriff rode to the ranch and arrested me for murder. I told him what had happened, but he didn't care—Jack Fields was his cousin! So he took me to town and locked me in jail to stand trial.

Uncle Bob got me a good lawyer. The circuit judge would be here in a week.

When the lawyer visited me, he asked, "Did the sheriff explain your rights to you when he arrested you?"

"No," I answered.

"Good! We can beat this," he replied.

One week later, the trial was held in the saloon. The judge called the court to order. The case was called. I pleaded not guilty.

My lawyer, Ed White, said, "Your Honor, we need to throw the case out. My client was not advised of his rights when he was arrested. He caught the victim robbing his uncle's safe!"

The judge asked me if I was advised of my rights when I was arrested.

"No, I was not," I answered.

He said, "Case dismissed!"

Uncle Bob told me to run and get in the wagon and ride fast and hard to the ranch and that he would follow.

"I want to make sure no one is following you. I expect trouble," he said.

I made it to the ranch safely. An hour later, Uncle Bob arrived at the ranch. He had to scare off some folks who didn't like the trial's outcome.

The next morning Uncle Bob got up early and saddled up a horse. He told me to leave Chicago.

He said, "You should stay away for at least a year for everything to calm down. Ride West—you may find your fortune out there! If not, return in a year, and you can try again. I love you, Max!"

"I love you too, Uncle Bob!" I said, and I was off.

CHAPTER 2

I started riding West through farmland and cattle ranches. I came to a little town called Rapid City, South Dakota. I had been riding for about a week. I went into the telegraph office and sent a telegram to my girlfriend, Susan Jones. I explained why I had to leave town so fast and would send for her when I got settled. I left the telegraph office and headed for the saloon when a gang of gunslingers came running from the bank.

Someone hollered, "The bank has been robbed! Get the sheriff! It's the James Gang!"

The sheriff came running with his gun drawn. He fired. Then Jesse James fired his gun, and the sheriff fell to the ground dead. With that, the gang rode out of town.

The deputy sheriff went around getting men to join his posse and go after the James Gang. I found myself in the posse. We trailed them for three days until we reached the Badlands, where the trail went cold. We camped for the night, and the next morning the posse disbanded.

I turned southeast for Dodge City. I went through an outpost trading center called Wall Drug. They had something great—ice water! And it was free! They also had the best ice cream I had ever tasted! While I was there, I heard some talk about carving presidents' heads into Mount Rushmore. What folly! The next day I got back on the road to Dodge City.

The nights were long and lonely. The coyotes kept me company. One night, a wolf came to visit me. He was hungry, so I fed him. He came back several nights, and we became friends. I named him Thor, after the Roman god of war.

We hit the road again. Thor was good at spotting the rattlesnakes and warning me. We had hot days and cold nights.

The next day we rode up on a cattle drive. I talked to the foreman, and they were a little short-handed on men, so I was hired on. At night I got to enjoy the company of the other drovers, and the free food was a bonus. I worked for them on the trail drive until we reached Kansas City.

I bought a newspaper and read what Horace Greeley wrote in the *Boston Globe* about the opportunities in the Western United States. It was called "Go West, Young Man," and it was picked up by newspapers nationwide. It told about the US government giving away free land to American citizens in the West just for settling on it and registering a claim in the US Land Office.

While I was reading the newspaper in the saloon, I started a conversation with a man named Steve Callahan. He was a logger and was headed to Seattle to do some logging. He said the Northwest Territories had enough trees to be logged for a thousand years!

He invited me to come with him to Seattle, Washington, and he would teach me how to log trees. We boarded a train for Seattle.

CHAPTER 3

W e arrived in Seattle on a wet Friday morning in July. I bought a house for $525 near Puget Sound with a great view. I then sent a telegram to Susan to come to Seattle and marry me. She sent a response back—YES! She arrived two weeks later! (That is how men get things done!)

I liked the logging industry. It took quite a while to get onto it. We cut down trees, cleared off the branches, and stacked the logs on wagons or ships. In the mountains, we would build a log flume to bring the logs down to the waters of Puget Sound, where we would float them down to the mill in Tacoma to be cut up into boards and sold.

Susan and I got married on August 6 in a little church in a glen in Seattle. We lived there for twelve years and were very happy. We had two boys, Ryan and Scotty. By this time, I was tired of logging. I had one accident at work where I took a twenty-foot fall when my strap broke. I hurt my back and was laid up for two months.

My gambling buddy, Joe Smith, had come to Seattle. I heard he was in town, so I went to see him at a saloon called Lilly's Place. I saw him playing cards at a table in the back. He recognized me when I approached the table and said, "As I live and breathe. Max, how have you been?"

"Fine!" I replied. He gave me a big hug. "Joe, are you in town long enough to give me a poker lesson? I will pay you ten bucks."

"How's tomorrow right here at noon? My serious work doesn't start until night."

"Thanks, Joe," I said, "let me buy you a beer."

"Okay," he said.

I asked him, "Where are you going from here?"

"New Orleans for Mardi Gras, and then gambling on a paddle-wheeler boat."

"Can you use a partner? I would like to go with you," I replied.

"I will think about it! If you do well tomorrow, we'll see!" he responded. I thanked him, and we finished our beers. I left, and Joe went back to his poker game.

The next morning, I couldn't wait to get to the saloon to start playing cards. I met with Joe, and he quizzed me on the game.

A cowboy came in, saw us working the cards, and said, "I want to play; deal me in!"

Joe said, "Okay, but it must be penny ante because I am trying to teach him the game."

The cowboy agreed, saying, "I can drink more beer that way."

Everything went fine for several hours. The cowboy got drunker and drunker. Joe taught me that you always wear a gun when you play cards. Suddenly, the cowboy flipped the table, called us cheats, and went for his gun. We all drew and fired. He fell dead on the floor.

As we left the saloon, we ran into an Army troop, and the colonel said, "Boys, you are in the Army now. You've been drafted!"

"But, sir, I have a bad back!" I protested.

"Does your trigger finger work?" he asked.

"Yes," I answered.

"Then you are in the US Army. Sergeant, get them uniforms!" he ordered.

Joe and I were in the Army at Fort Dix for the next two years. The Army taught us firearms safety under the direction of General Custer:

Always point your gun at the ground or in the air when not planning to fire it.

Don't aim a gun at someone unless you plan to shoot them.

If you fire a gun, shoot to kill.

Don't pull out a gun unless you want to fire it.

The food was awful! K-rations. It was a dark time in our lives, but we survived! I was glad when my two years were over, and I was a free man again.

I returned to Seattle to see my family before heading off to New Orleans to start my new career as a gambler. It was nice being home. I went back to logging for a while. I stayed about a year; then it was off to New Orleans. I rode my favorite horse, Lucky.

It was a hot day as I rode along, and I was sweating like a pig. I saw a sign that read 75 miles to Kansas City, so I turned east and went that way. Finally, I reached the small town of Des Moines, Iowa. I went into the saloon for a drink. I walked up to the bar and ordered a beer.

The bartender asked me if I would be in town for a while.

I said, "Yes."

He advised me that the hotel was two blocks down the street where I could get a room with a bath. It was 101 degrees. A good bath makes you feel better in that heat. Also, the hotel had a good restaurant in it.

I asked him, "Do you want to hire a gambler as a part of your saloon?"

"Maybe, check back with me tomorrow."

"Okay," I replied.

I went to the hotel, checked in, and got a bath. Later I went for a pork chop dinner with all the trimmings, then I went to bed. The next day after breakfast, I went to the saloon and talked to the owner. He agreed to stake me and pay 25% of my winnings. The house takes 75%.

I said, "Okay, I will try it for a while."

He said to be there by noon to start.

"I will see you then," I replied.

I went to the Sears department store and bought a suit and two fancy shirts for work. I went back to the hotel to change clothes and went back to the saloon to start work. I won most of the hands and had a lot of fun and success. After a few weeks, who walked into the saloon but Joe Smith.

We hugged, and he said, "I thought you were coming to New Orleans!"

"I got sidetracked," I explained to him.

We played blackjack and poker for a few weeks with the locals and a few cowboys who blew through town. Finally, Joe got bored and told me he was headed for New Orleans.

I said, "I will see you there in a few weeks. Save me a seat at the tables."

CHAPTER 4

I t was early fall by then, and a nip was in the air. As I walked past the train station, I saw some men unloading a lot of cattle and horses.

I hollered, "Hey, what's up?"

"The rodeo has come to town," they replied.

"That sounds like fun," I answered.

The rodeo crew came into the bar for a drink. I approached them, introduced myself, and asked if I could try a few events.

"Anyone can compete. All they have to do is register, pay the $5 entrance fee, and sign up for the events they wish to compete in."

"That's it?" I said.

"Yep! That's it," they replied.

The day came for the rodeo, and I went early to the fairgrounds, where the rodeo was held, paid my entrance fee, and signed up for bronco busting and bull riding. After that, I went to lunch and then back to the fairgrounds.

The rodeo started with the national anthem. They called the bull riding event first. I drew a ride on a bull called Rocket. I climbed on his back, they opened the gate, and we were off. He bucked like nothing I had ever seen before! I stayed on for ten seconds. (You only needed to stay on for eight seconds.) When I got off, I heard my back snap. I fell to the ground and was carried out of the arena.

When I got backstage, I felt better! After a few minutes of resting, I was fine. I won my event. The next event was women's barrel racing. Then came my next event, which was bronco busting. I drew Volcano. He was one mean horse. When the gate opened, I lasted two seconds—he threw me up ten feet in the air. I landed in a bunch of horse shit. It broke my fall, but boy, did I stink! I took three baths to get it all off me. I won $1,000 and a gold buckle for bull riding. I was invited to go to the rodeo in two weeks in San Antonio, Texas. It was a big one run by Will Rogers.

The next morning, I started riding for Texas. It was hot and dusty on the trail. I rode to Denver and caught a train to San Antonio. The trip was uneventful, and I reached San Antonio three days later. I was dying to see the Alamo. It was an incredible sight, and I spent two days checking it out. The next day, after breakfast, I went looking for a poker game. In the Purple Lady Saloon, I got into a poker game where I won several hands. I walked away with $500.

The day of the rodeo came, and I met Will Rogers at the arena when I went to register for my events. He is a great guy! I entered three events: bull riding, bronco busting, and bulldogging. The rodeo started with the princesses riding in with the colors and then the national anthem. The bull riding event was first. I drew Torres. I climbed on, and the gate opened. I made it for eight seconds. Women's barrel racing was next. Will Rogers did some fancy rope tricks, and then it was time for the bulldogging.

The calf was released, and I took off after him on my horse to rope and tie him as quickly as possible. I got 5.5 seconds. I came in second in this event. I also came in third in the bull riding event. After a few more of Will Rogers' tricks and storytelling, it came to my favorite event—bronco busting. I drew Thunder Mountain. I climbed on his back, the gate opened, and we were off. I only lasted five seconds. I concluded that rodeo was not for me.

The next morning, I left for New Orleans on horseback. When I reached Dallas, Texas, I heard that a new game was being played there called "Baseball." Abner Doubleday had two teams playing each other: the Texas Rangers and the Chicago Cubs. I bought a ticket for 50 cents.

It was a lot of fun. Babe Ruth hit a home run! What a game! Chicago won 5 to 3. The next morning, I left on my horse on the long ride to New Orleans. It was a hot, muggy day, and I missed my family. It took the rest of the day to get across Texas. I made camp just outside Lake Charles, Louisiana.

The next day after breakfast, I finished my ride into New Orleans. I got a hotel room in the French Quarter. That night I went clubbing. I love Jazz Music! What a night. I heard the great Louis Armstrong. (Man, could he play the trumpet). The next night I went to the Top

Hat Club and heard Al Hirt on the trumpet. I ran into Joe Smith at the club. We talked for a while over a beer, and Joe was going to meet me at the hotel at 8:00 a.m. and take me to the riverboat.

The Andrew Jackson was a 300-foot paddle-wheeler. Joe introduced me to Mat Johnson, the captain and owner of the riverboat.

Joe said, "Captain Mat, I need you to hire my friend Max Seagle as one of your gamblers. He is my partner and can help me double your winnings!"

Captain Mat agreed.

"Max, 20% of your winnings is yours, and I keep the rest. I will stake you at $500 at the beginning of your shift. You will work 12-hour shifts, sleep on the boat, and get two days off when we are in port. Your cabin is number P200. Welcome Aboard! We cast off in two hours, so get some rest. Our passengers will start arriving in about an hour," said Captain Mat.

Two hours later, the crew cast off, and the Andrew Jackson was on its way. Joe and I got set up in the casino and worked from the same table playing seven-card stud poker. The first night we took the suckers for $25,000. Captain Mat was amazed!

The next day I was dealing blackjack, and Joe played five-card draw poker. I won $1,200. The passengers were running out of money. Captain Mat landed the ship back in New Orleans. We got two days off. I sent a telegram to my family informing them of my exploits. I received an answer from my wife that she wanted to join me.

I went to talk to Captain Mat about my situation. He advised me that the ship was not a suitable environment for kids. He suggested I buy them a house in New Orleans, and I could see them on my days off. So, I told her to sell the house in Seattle and come to New Orleans. Three weeks later, they arrived. It was great to see my family. My boys had really grown since I last saw them. We bought a house for them and got them moved in. We put the boys in school, and I went back to work.

Susan had the idea to bring her parents from Chicago and relocate them to New Orleans so they could watch the boys, and she could go on the ship with me. We discussed it and decided to do it. Her parents were thrilled with the idea. They could see Susan and the grandkids more often. A few weeks later, they arrived. We helped them find a house and settle in.

The next morning, I took Susan on board the ship. She toured the paddle wheeler and loved it. We cast off and went to sea. Joe and I both dealt blackjack at different tables. I lost $2,000 in the first hour. After that, I traded tables with Joe, and my luck changed. Over the next eight hours, I won $5,000. When my shift ended, I went to my stateroom, where Susan was waiting for me. I told her I loved her, and we went to bed. The next morning, we ate breakfast in the ship's restaurant, where we had eggs, bacon, toast, and coffee. Then I went to work.

I was playing five-card draw poker, and I won almost every hand. Joe asked me how I got on such a hot winning streak. I told him, "It's in the genes!"

The next few weeks were uneventful, but as we docked the boat, I saw a circus tent a few blocks from the pier.

As we left the ship, arm in arm, I said to Sue, "Let's take the boys to the circus."

It was the Barnum and Bailey Circus. The Greatest Show on Earth was in town.

Sue said, "That's a great idea! We will all go!"

We went home and told the kids, and they were thrilled.

Saturday came, and it was off to the circus. Susan's parents loved the elephants. I never saw a man stick his head in a lion's mouth before. He was crazy! The boys liked the clowns. Susan liked the tightrope walkers. I bought the kids pink cotton candy and Coca-Cola. The circus workers let us feed the elephants when the show was over, and we all had fun.

CHAPTER 5

A s we were casting off on a day in May, the ship's engine made a horrible grinding sound and a loud bang. A gear fell off the paddle wheel into the bay. We were about 75 feet from the shore. The Harbor Patrol towed us in, and Captain Mat sent for the mechanic. When the mechanic got there, it was late afternoon. He went right to work. He fixed the engine but needed some parts to fix the paddle wheel. He sent a telegram to Kansas City to the parts supply house. He got a reply back. They had the parts he needed, but the stagecoach from New Orleans was not scheduled to leave for five days.

Captain Mat said, "We can't wait!"

He asked me to take a wagon to Kansas City to get the parts. Joe volunteered to go with me on the trip. The next morning, we were off. We had to go through Indian territory on the way. It took us two days to get there. We went to the parts warehouse, paid for the parts, and loaded the wagon. We went to the saloon and had a drink. After we each had a beer, we headed for home.

We went through Dodge City, where we spent the night. We went to the Long Branch Saloon for a beer.

I got into a five-card draw poker game. I won $500. Then I went to bed. Joe was still drinking when I left the saloon. A while later, I heard a gunshot. Joe had gotten into a poker game and drew a full house from the dealer. One of the cowboys accused Joe of cheating. He drew his gun, and Joe shot him dead with his Derringer. The bartender called the marshal. Marshal Matt Dillon came and arrested Joe for murder. The next day, Miss Kitty, the owner of the Long Branch Saloon, came to Joe's aid. One of her girls saw the whole thing and said it was a fair fight.

When they released Joe, he ran for the wagon and drove out of town as fast as he could. He forgot about me and left without me. I bought a horse at the livery stable and headed for home by way of Tombstone, Arizona. I wanted to see the town and play poker there.

• • •

I had some hot and lonely days and nights on the road. One night a coyote came into my camp. He was starving, so I gave him some of my canned chili and water. I was surprised he liked my chili! I named him Scout. He went with me on the trail.

It took an additional two days to reach Tombstone. When I got there, who was there to greet me but none other than the famous Bat Masterson, the sheriff of Tombstone. I told him I was a tourist and a gambler. He collected my guns and said I could have them back when I left town. I got a room for the night at the hotel and went to the Kitty Cat Saloon to play poker. I got into a game with beginners. I beat them three hands straight, cashed in my chips, drank my beer, and went to the can-can show at the saloon down the street. It was a good show. I enjoyed it and went to my hotel room.

The next morning, I got into a good poker game that lasted all day and into the night. I won $2,500. I went to the can-can show one more time. I had planned to head home the next day.

After breakfast the next day, I went to the sheriff's office, collected my guns, and started on my ride home. Scout was still with me.

CHAPTER 6

I rode to the crest of the Grand Canyon. It was a breathtaking view! I sat there for about an hour, resting and enjoying the view before getting back on the road.

I rode into Indian country, where I made camp for the night. After daybreak, I made breakfast for Scout and me, broke camp, and started riding. Scout was skittish. Just then, as I was riding through the desert, an Indian scouting party saw me, and the arrows started flying. I kept riding, and to my amazement, no arrows hit me. The Indians rode up to me, and one jumped me, knocking me from my horse. We fought, and he knocked me out. They took me to their camp and tied me up inside a teepee. Then who walked in but the Chief, Sitting Bull. He asked me what I was doing on their land.

"Just riding through on my way home," I told Him.

"We don't like the white man. He speaks with a forked tongue! Bury him up to his neck in an ant hill!" he said, and the lights went out.

I woke up buried to my neck in the dirt and couldn't move. A brave walked by, and I begged him to get the Chief.

"Please get me the Chief. I need a pow-wow with him! Help!" I hollered.

He went and got Sitting Bull.

Sitting Bull came and said, "What do you want? What are your last words?"

"Do you want to get even with the white man? I know how—by taking his money away. Through gambling! That's poker, blackjack, and other games of chance. I am a gambler. I can help you, but not if I'm dead."

He told his braves to dig me up and clean me up for our pow-wow. Next, his braves took me to a nearby river for a bath. I enjoyed my bath while the Indian women washed my clothes. Then, I was ushered into a tribal banquet. The food was excellent—salmon, potatoes, and corn. Sitting Bull told the tribe they would celebrate tonight and talk with the tribe elders and me tomorrow. Then, the drums and dances started, and we partied late into the night.

The morning came, and after breakfast, we met in Sitting Bull's teepee.

Sitting Bull looked at me and said, "Tell us your plan."

I said, "We need to build a casino. It needs many tables—one for each game. It needs to be a nice place. The Indian dealers have to dress up in white men's suits."

Sitting Bull interrupted me and asked, "Why do we need to do this?"

"We are trying to get the white man to come and bring his money! Games of chance are set up to favor the house—that's us. As we get money, we add carpeting, a fancy bar for alcoholic drinks served by beautiful women, and slot machines. We need a few people to win to balance out the losses. We want the winners to go home and tell their friends how much fun they had here. We need to add a restaurant for food. Does the tribe have any gold or white man's money to buy building materials to build the casino?"

Sitting Bull said, "We have some bags of gold."

I replied, "Good! Send one of your braves with me to order the bricks, and when they come in, we will build the casino in those trees over there. The shade will cool the building. We will build a stage and create a can-can show many moons from now. When the Indians are working in the casino, they can't drink alcohol! I will teach your people how to deal cards. We will set up a cashier's cage for the money. We will make a lot of money!"

The elders wanted me to demonstrate my card skills, so I gave them a quick demonstration. Then they asked me to leave the tent so they could talk. About an hour later, Sitting Bull came to me and said we had a deal, and the tribe would build the casino.

When morning came, Sitting Bull chose one of his braves, Speedy Horse, to go with me into Flagstaff to order the building materials we needed to build the casino. Speedy Horse carried the gold. When we got to town, we went to the general store and found two wagons full of red brick and two full of concrete blocks and mortar. We bought them all. I drove one of the wagons, Speedy Horse drove a wagon, and the store owner had two clerks drive the other two wagons.

Sitting Bull and his braves unloaded the wagons when we got to the camp. I drew up some plans for the casino while two of Sitting Bull's braves helped return the wagons. I had taken some classes in architecture while at Harvard. When the braves got back from town, we had started to pour the foundation of the building. It went well, and we finished by sundown. We let the foundation dry and cure for three days.

Then we started framing the building. The construction went slowly. We got glass windows from St. Louis. We built trusses and put them up. We got tile roofing from California. We had fun getting the roof on straight. The braves were hard workers. The casino was taking shape, and Sitting Bull was delighted.

We ordered the best carpet from Chicago. It was gorgeous! We bought flushing toilets from New York City. I installed a 16" pipe in the waterfall. Fifty feet down the line, I went to a 12" diagonal pipe. Another fifty feet downline, I changed to a 6" diameter pipe that I ran into the casino. I broke it out to a ½" pipe to the toilets and sinks. This gave me the water pressure I needed to get the toilets to flush. Once installed, they worked fine. We imported the slot machines from Monte Carlo.

Our casino had its grand opening on July 4, 1899. It was a great day—fireworks, a parade, the works! General Custer came to the grand opening. A few days later, he got into a poker game with me. He lost $500 to me (the house). After that, he had dinner in the restaurant and then went to the can-can show. The next afternoon, he asked for a $5,000 line of credit. I told him I would have to discuss it with my partner, Sitting Bull.

Sitting Bull asked, "Is he good for it?"

"I am not sure. I know there has been some talk he could be the next President of the United States," I responded.

"Do it. I will kill him if he loses and can't pay it back."

I went to General Custer and advised him, "We will give you a $ 5,000 line of credit, provided you can pay it back!"

He said, "No problem!"

I signed his marker and gave it to him.

One hour later, he joined a poker game I was running. He won the first hand. The pot was $500. He ordered a whiskey, and shortly after that, his luck began to change. He lost the next five hands. We broke up the game for dinner and the can-can show. I was helping out that night in the Lucky Aces Restaurant. We had a busy night. The next morning after breakfast, General Custer asked me when my next poker game was.

I replied, "About 2:00 p.m. We have other dealers if you don't want to wait.

"No, that's fine!" he said.

At 2:00, I set up a high-stakes poker game in the casino—$100 buy-in. General Custer joined us. We had two wealthy cattlemen and an oil tycoon. I asked the general if he could afford to play in this game and let him know that I would be running a regular game tonight with a $5 buy-in.

He said, "No, this game suits me fine."

Sitting Bull came in to watch the game. We anteed up, and I started dealing the cards. The general won the first hand with a king-high straight. The cattlemen won the following two hands. On the next hand, the oil tycoon raised the bet to $1,000, and then General Custer raised another $5,000. The cattlemen folded. The oil man took one card, and General Custer stood pat. The oil man raised his bet $1,000, and General Custer signed another marker for $1,000. The oil man had a straight, General Custer had a full house, and I had a royal flush, winning the hand.

Sitting Bull told General Custer it was time to pay the $6,000 he owed the casino. His braves (our security men) took him out back, and Sitting Bull went with them. We added two more players, and the game resumed. We played for three more hours, and then we broke for dinner. I went out back to find General Custer. What I found surprised me: General Custer was dead with a dozen arrows sticking out of him. I went and found Sitting Bull and asked him what happened.

"He couldn't pay his debt!" answered Sitting Bull.

"This is terrible! We can't let his body be found here!" I exclaimed.

Sitting Bull said, "I know. Put his body in a wagon and take it north to Montana to our cousins' land. The Indians are at war with the white man. When they find his body, they will think he was a casualty of war."

"I like it!" I exclaimed.

So that's what they did. On their way to Montana, the Indians ran across a Cavalry scout troop. The Indians shot them with arrows, put their bodies in the wagon with General Custer, and continued to Montana. They found a nice open spot by a river and dumped the bodies. (Today, that land is known as Custer's Battlefield).

When the braves returned from Montana, Sitting Bull and I asked them how it went. They told us what they had done. We asked them why the extra men.

"So we could stage it like a real battle," they answered.

A few weeks later, we got a copy of the San Francisco newspaper reporting the heroic death of General Custer. It made a great story, but we knew the truth.

CHAPTER 7

A few months later, President Ulysses S. Grant came to our casino for a visit. Our casino was the talk of Washington, D.C. He loved our casino, especially the bar where he spent several hours. He attended our can-can show every night. We got acquainted in the bar and became good friends.

A few days later, he got into a high-stakes poker game I was dealing. Lady Luck was with him and he won $10,000. The next day, I heard a rumor that President Grant had returned to Washington, D.C.

He turned up at our casino a week later after a hunting trip. He had shot a three-point buck elk. Several hours later, I ran into President Grant in the bar, and he told me the whole story. It goes as follows: President Grant was reminded by his Secretary of War that General Custer bragged for years about a hunting trip he went on in Colorado where he shot a 1,000-pound buffalo. So he said, "Let's go hunting around Lake Tahoe." So we did! It took us two days to get there to Lake Tahoe. We left our horses with one of my aids and proceeded on foot. That night we made camp on the north side of the lake. We were up at dawn and hiked to the west side of the lake. There we lay in wait for an elk to come and drink.

Around 7:00 p.m., we got our chance—a three-point buck came to the water for a drink. I aimed and fired, and he took off on a run. We tracked him for 500 yards, where we found him dead. I sent an aide for the horses while we dressed out the carcass. The next morning, we started back to the casino. It took us another two and a half days to get back. Now I have a story for the ages!

President Grant said, "I am tired! I am going to stay here for a few days to rest up before I return to Washington."

"That is fine, Mr. President!" I exclaimed.

He went to our dinner smorgasbord and can-can show. After the show, he turned in for the night.

About noon the next day, I started a high-stakes poker game. To my surprise, President Grant joined us. The first hand went to the cattle baron with a king-high straight. President Grant won the next two hands. The game continued until 1:00 a.m. After that, we quit for the night. I got a ribeye steak dinner and went to bed.

I took the next day off and met my wife, who surprised me with a visit. I took her for a picnic by the river. We went for a horseback ride in the country and then for a swim in the river. We had a great time! The next day I took her to the train station and sent her home to New Orleans. Later, I ran into President Grant in the bar. He had been drinking for hours. He wanted to play poker. I told him I would start a game at 8:00 p.m. after the can-can show. I told the bartender to cut the

President off, start serving him coffee, and get him a ham sandwich.

At 7:15 p.m., the high-stakes poker game began. President Grant won the first hand with a full house. He ordered a boilermaker from the bar, and I won the next two hands. Then President Grant, after the deal, wanted me to bet the casino. I told him no. He insisted, so I went and got my partner, Sitting Bull. I told him what the President wanted. He sat at the table with us and said, "If I do that and you lose, I want to own the states of Nevada and Arizona!"

President Grant said, "I will put up the twelve western states."

"Okay," said Sitting Bull.

The President stayed pat. I took one card. President Grant had an ace-high straight, but I had a royal flush in hearts. I won the hand. Sitting Bull took President Grant to his office to get the deed drawn up for ownership to the twelve western states of the United States. After the papers were signed, President Grant went to his room and then to bed.

The next day, President Grant asked me if Congress could buy back the twelve western states. I said I would talk to Sitting Bull. So I went to Sitting Bull and told him that President Grant wanted to get Congress to repurchase the twelve western states from us that he lost in the poker game.

"I think we should let them repurchase them for $1 million in gold for each state," said Sitting Bull.

"Okay, I will tell him," I said, then went and told President Grant.

He said, "I will see what I can do and send you a telegram."

The next morning, President Grant caught a train back to Washington, D.C.

I told Sitting Bull it is time to take some of our money and start a new casino in the Nevada desert. Something bigger, brighter, and better. We could even start our own town and call it Las Vegas!

Sitting Bull said, "Okay, you go and build it, and I will run this casino. If you need help, send for me."

"Thanks!" I answered. *I am finally free*, I thought to myself.

I packed up my things and got on my horse and left. I stopped in Carson City and sent telegrams to suppliers to order what I needed to start my new casino in Las Vegas—The Flamingo Casino. I hired a construction crew and started building.

Meanwhile, back in Washington, D.C., President Grant had his own problems. He had to confess what he had done to Congress and convince them to give him $12,000,000 in gold to repurchase the 12 western states from Sitting Bull. President Grant finally got the money from Congress. The next day, he boarded a train going West and arrived at the casino five days later. He gave the gold to Sitting Bull, and he had him sign the deed to the western states back to the United States government. The next day President Grant got on a train back to Washington, D.C.

After that, Sitting Bull sent me five million dollars' worth of gold bars to help finish and open my casino in Las Vegas. Six months later, I opened The Flamingo

Casino. We had fireworks, and several Hollywood stars came as our guests. It was a great success! The housing industry was booming with all the new employees at the casino. We even had a Sears department store. The town of Las Vegas was becoming a city!

CHAPTER 8

After establishing Las Vegas, I heard about a gold strike in Alaska. I always wanted to pan for gold. So the following day, I bought a ticket on a ship to Sitka, Alaska. It took three days to get there. When I arrived, I went to the general store to buy my supplies and set out for the site. I filed a claim and started panning for gold. After four hours, I stopped to set up the camp.

The next morning after breakfast, I started digging and filtering dirt and panning for gold. This went on for a month, and then I struck it rich. I found a rock five inches round that was 95% gold. I started building my mine. I dug out more and more gold. After a few weeks, I hired a mining crew. I lived in Alaska for two years.

The gold was running out. Late one night, I set off a dynamite charge to find a new ore vein, but oil bubbled up. I was rich again! The bottom of the mine filled up with oil. I sent for oil pumping equipment. It took two months to arrive. I also ordered drilling equipment, with which I established the Texaco Oil & Gas Company.

One night after dinner and drinks, I stumbled out of my favorite watering hole and heard strange music from a giant circus tent. I wandered over to it to see what was going on. It was some kind of church camp meeting. Dr. Brazee was holding services there. He preached salvation through the death and resurrection of Jesus Christ (God's one and only Son). He told us we could have our sins forgiven and someday make Heaven our home. At the end of the service, he gave an altar call, and I went forward and gave my life to Jesus Christ as my Lord and Savior.

Soon after that, I received a telegram from my son, Scott. My wife had taken ill and died. I was needed at home. I vowed not to leave home again. I ran the oil company from my office in Las Vegas.

CHAPTER 9

Santa Anna, the President of Mexico, visited me in Las Vegas.

"Max," he said, "I want to get into the gambling trade. Can you help me?"

"Yes. Do you have any trained dealers?" I asked.

"No," he replied.

"No problem. I can train your people. Where do you want to put your casino?"

"I don't know. Where do you suggest?"

"If you did it here in Las Vegas, you would have to deal with the mob, but you own a little Caribbean Island called Cuba; I suggest you invest in building two casinos to start with. Make them picturesque by the seashore with a bar and stage for big shows like can-can dance shows. Keep the price for rooms and food cheap; you can make up the difference in gambling. I will sell you the plans we used to build The Flamingo," I told him.

"How much?" he asked.

"One hundred dollars. I am not out to make money on you, my friend," I advised him.

He replied, "Good! That's real good!"

"There are ten sets of plans we used through the years," I said. So I gave him my plans, we finished our business, and he left for Mexico City.

• • •

One day Al Capone visited and asked me how he could set up and control gambling worldwide. I told him, "I don't know about around the world, but you and your partners can build many casinos here in Las Vegas."

"How many do you think we need?" he asked.

"I think about twelve to fifteen should do it," I told him. "My people and I can teach your people how to deal and run other games of chance.

Al said, "That sounds fine!"

"After we get our fifteen casinos built, we will need to advertise Las Vegas as a fun, family-friendly resort town," Al told me.

The following day Al caught a train back to Chicago. A few weeks later, construction crews were everywhere. It took two years to complete the new casinos on one street that would become known as The Strip. The Mob had arrived!

I met Sam James, an avid fisherman, in the bar of The Flamingo Casino. We became friends. He said, "Let's go fishing tomorrow."

"Where?" I asked.

"Lake Powell. I will meet you in the lobby at 5:00 a.m.," he said.

"Okay," I replied.

I met him, and we got into his pickup truck and drove five hours to Lake Powell. We launched his twenty-foot fiberglass boat with a hundred-horse Mercury outboard motor and a twenty-five-horse fishing motor. We got in the boat, fixed our lines, and dropped them in the lake. We started trolling. After about an hour, Sam got a bite. The fish stole his worm off his hook, so he rebaited his hook and cast it back into the lake.

About ten minutes later, a three-pound bass hit his line; he fought it for twenty minutes to get it into the boat. A half-hour later, I caught my first fish. It was a two-pound bass that was 12" long. Sam caught two more before we quit for the day at about 4:00 p.m. After that, we pulled the boat out of the water and returned to Las Vegas. I got home at about 9:30 at night. We had a great time.

Sam said, "We should go deer hunting this fall."

"That sounds like fun! Let's do it," I exclaimed.

• • •

Just after Max's 80th birthday, he disappeared from The Flamingo Casino and was never seen again. It was believed that the mob killed him and buried him in the desert outside of Las Vegas.

Shortly after Max's disappearance, the mob bought The Flamingo Casino.

Max's sons believe his sins from the past had caught up with him!

THE END

THE FOX'S TAIL

Once upon a time, there was a family of foxes. Sammy was the youngest of the family. He had a big sister by the name of Susan. He had a loving mother, Barbara. Sammy's father was a hardworking Dad by the name of Bill.

It was daybreak in The Great Woods. Barbara let the little ones know it was time for breakfast. She made them scrambled eggs and bacon with toast and jam and milk. Bill came in and said, "Good Morning."

After breakfast, Barbara told her kids to brush their teeth. After they had finished getting ready for school, she sent them on their way. She kissed Bill goodbye and sent him off to work at a construction company in the town of Sunrise. Then, she washed the dishes and continued cleaning their den.

At school, Sammy's teacher, Mrs. Jill Smith (also a fox), told him he got an "A" in fishing class.

"You caught your first rainbow trout, and you are doing well in gathering and counting nuts," she said.

Later that day, Mrs. Smith told her class, "Students, it is very important to know the concept of Survival of the

Fittest! The weak, injured, and elderly get eaten by wicked beasts here in The Great Woods. Those are the creatures that eat smaller animals for food. Don't be the meat! Protect yourselves and your friends in times of danger!"

She continued, "There are many dangers in The Great Woods: man, bears, wolves, owls, hawks, and eagles, just to mention a few. If you run into a bear, freeze, stand still, and hope he doesn't see you. If he heads your way—RUN! Run as fast as you can to the bushes and take cover!"

On Saturday mornings, Bill's day off, he goes out hunting for meat for the family. That day, he caught a rabbit for dinner. Meanwhile, Barbara took the kids to the supermarket to buy food.

One day, on the way home from school, Sammy ran across a giant Grizzly Bear. The bear roared and charged him. Sammy was scared and started to run as fast as he could, but the bear quickly caught up to him. Sammy thought it was curtains! The bear swatted Sammy with his big paw, and Sammy went flying. He landed in a big heap, bleeding from his wounds. He played dead. The bear sniffed him, and thinking Sammy was dead, he went on his way. Jake, the wolf, found Sammy, picked him up, and carried him home.

Barbara exclaimed, "Sammy, What happened to you! She laid him on his bed, washed and bandaged his wounds. She thanked Jake for bringing Sammy home and sent him on his way. She nursed Sammy back to health. A few weeks later, Sammy's friends Scotty the deer and Jake the wolf came to his house for a sleepover. They were BFFs (Best Friends Forever).

On the way to school, Sammy encountered a young cougar. The cougar said, "Give me all your money!"

Sammy shouted, "NO! I am on my way to school and need my lunch money!"

The cougar jumped him, and they fought. Sammy was getting beaten up. He cried out, "HELP! HELP!"

Then, to his amazement, who should appear but Mighty Mouse who exclaimed, "There is no need to fear! Mighty Mouse is here! Here I come to save the day!"

Mighty Mouse swooped in and started beating the daylights out of that cougar.

The cougar cried out, "STOP! STOP! You are hurting me!"

Mighty Mouse said, "Have you learned your lesson? Bullying is not permitted in The Great Woods! If you do this again, I will put you in jail!"

The cougar said, "I won't do it again. I am sorry!"

Mighty Mouse flew away, and Sammy went on to school. When he got there, he told everyone what happened.

Mrs. Smith told the class, "Mighty Mouse was right! NO bullying anywhere! It is not acceptable behavior!"

Several days later, Sammy and Jake went off playing in the woods. After several hours, they started getting hungry. Jake said, "Let's go to Farmer Jones's place and raid the chicken coop. I love fried chicken!"

So they snuck onto the farm and into the chicken coop. The chicken started making noise, but Jake grabbed one and said, "Let's go!"

As they left the coop, Farmer Jones showed up with his shotgun. A loud BANG! BANG! rang out, and Jake was dead. Mighty Mouse heard the shots, swooped in to grab Sammy, and flew him home. (Sammy was safe). Mighty Mouse told Barbara and Bill what had happened. They scolded Sammy and told him what he did was wrong.

"You can't steal Farmer Jones's chickens," said Mighty Mouse.

Sammy's parents said, "Sammy, you know stealing is wrong! You heard Pastor John say so at church last Sunday."

Mighty Mouse flew away, and the Fox family went into the house for dinner.

Later that evening, Bill said to the kids, "Tomorrow is Bring Your Kids to Work Day. Would you like to go to work with me?"

Sammy and Susan said, "Yes, Dad! That sounds like fun!"

Barbara said, "Bill, are you sure the construction site is safe?"

"Yes. It is safe!"

The next morning, Bill and the kids went to work together. The boss brought a bounce house, a Ferris Wheel, and a merry-go-round. They got to see the construction project. The company had soda pop and ice cream and a nice lunch. It was a fun day for all.

On the way home, Bill asked his kids if they would like to go on a picnic on Sunday. "Yes, it sounds like a grand idea," they said.

On Sunday, they went to church and then to Deer Park for their picnic. After a nice meal, they went to the ice cream vendor and bought ice cream bars. Then, they spent the rest of the day playing games in the park before going home.

• • •

Bill told his family one spring morning in May, "No one goes outside today or leaves the house! According to the paperboy, this is Fox Hunting Day. He told me when I went to get the newspaper. If a fox comes to the door, let him in quickly; he may have dogs on his trail or a hunter."

At 9:00 a.m., a bugle sounded, and they heard a shout, "Tally Ho!" followed by the sound of dogs barking. Hours later, there was a BANG! BANG!, nothing for a while, and then the sound of barking dogs. A little bit later, there was a faint knock at the door. It was a half-dead fox. He said, "Help!" They let him in. He was bleeding from three wounds.

Bill said, "I can get the pellets out from two of these wounds easily, but the third one is deep. What is your name, son?"

"My name is Peter. Please do what you can."

So Bill went to work, and soon two pellets from the gunshot wounds were out.

Bill told Barbara, "You had better do the deep wound."

Barbara used to be a nurse. So she went right to work. Before long, she had the pellet out. She bandaged Peter's wounds, and during the next few weeks, Barbara nursed him back to health. Then, when Peter was well enough, he left for home.

• • •

One night in the middle of winter, Sammy woke up from hibernation and could not go back to sleep, so he woke his mother and told her he had forgotten to bring home his homework for the hibernation break. She said, "You can go get it now if you want to. The school is unlocked during the break, and I will go with you."

So they set off for the school. The moon was full and bright to light their way. They got to the school, and Sammy got his book. The assignment was still on the whiteboard. Sammy copied it down, and they were on their way back home. A spotted owl was watching them. The owl thought they would make a good meal. As he made his move and swooped down to grab them, they heard, "Here I Come To Save The Day!" It was Mighty Mouse! He flew in, and POW! he knocked the owl to the ground with one blow.

Mighty Mouse checked with Sammy and Barbara to see if they were all right. They said they were fine. They thanked Mighty Mouse! He picked up the owl and carried him out of The Great Woods—for the owl to never return. Sammy and his mother arrived home safely. Barbara then put Sammy to bed to continue their hibernation. "If you wake up again, you may do your homework," she said; Barbara also returned to bed.

A few weeks later, a new family of foxes moved into The Great Woods named Adams. They had a young fox by the name of Tommy. Sammy and Tommy became good friends.

One day Sammy saw in the newspaper that NASA would put a man on Mars.

Sammy said, "Mom, I want to go with them to Mars!"

Barbara said, "You can't!"

"Why not?" Sammy asked.

His Dad said, "They won't have any food for you, and there is no oxygen in Outer Space for you to breathe."

Sammy said, "I don't care!"

Bill shouted, "Go to your room, and we will hear no more about it!"

The next day, Sammy told Tommy he wanted to sneak onto the rocket to Mars.

Tommy said, "That sounds like fun! I'm in!"

Sammy said, "We have a week to get to Florida before they launch the rocket."

Tommy said, "A freight train comes through here tomorrow at midnight, bound for Florida."

"We can make that! Get as much food as you can carry," Sammy replied.

"We will meet at the train station in Sunnyside at 11:00 p.m. tomorrow," Tommy agreed.

The next night the two foxes sneaked out and met at the train station as planned. They found the train, made their way onto an empty boxcar, and fell fast asleep. They were well on their way to Florida when they woke the next morning.

Two days later, they arrived in Central Florida. It was easy to see the rocket miles away because Florida is very flat. They proceeded to the skywalk, looking for a ride to the cape. They saw a tourist bus that read "Cape Kennedy" on its reader screen. They jumped from the skywalk onto the top of the bus, where they had a scenic ride to the cape. When they reached Cape Kennedy (also known as Cape Canaveral), they ran over to the elevator, proceeded to the top of the rocket, slipped into the Space Shuttle Atlantis, and hid.

The following day, the five astronauts were loaded onto the Space Shuttle Atlantis, and the countdown to the launch began. The launch was perfect, and Atlantis was on its way to Mars.

Two days later, the two foxes came out of hiding, scaring the astronauts. They welcomed the foxes as the first pets in space. James, head of the mission, called Houston to inform them of the stowaways. Sammy and Tommy made the national news that night. Their families heard about it and were very distressed about their little foxes' actions.

Barbara went searching for Mighty Mouse. She found him at the edge of The Great Woods. She told him what Sammy and Tommy had done. Mighty Mouse said, "That is a long flight. It will take me a week to reach Mars and another week to return to Earth. I recommend watching the news, and if everything goes all right with the space mission, just wait until they get back, but if you need me to go get them—I will!"

Barbara said, "Thank You! I will let you know!" and returned home.

The space mission was proceeding without a hitch. One month later, the space shuttle arrived and started orbiting Mars. The next day, the astronauts entered the shuttle bay and prepared to launch the Land Rover lander to the surface of the red planet. Two astronauts, along with Tommy and Sammy, entered the landing module. The shuttle bay doors opened, the lander's engines fired up, and they were on their way to the surface of Mars. One hour later, they made a bumpy landing on the surface. One of the landing module's engines broke off upon impact. The two astronauts, Pete and Jill, informed James, who was in the space shuttle, of the problem.

James said, "I am not sure you can escape the planet's gravitational pull with just one engine! I will inform NASA. Good Luck! Proceed with your mission experiments, plant seeds, and gather rock samples.

"Okay, we will!" said Pete. They wanted to see if there was enough moisture to grow corn and wheat on Mars. They spent three days planting seeds and gathering samples. Then, when they were ready to leave the surface of Mars, they started the engine, and the craft began to move. Before long, the engine gave out. They hadn't gotten off the surface more than three feet. It landed with a thud. It was too heavy for one engine alone.

Jill called James on the radio and yelled, "Help! What do we do now?"

James said, "Let the engine rest a while and try again. Leave any extra rock samples to lighten the load. Pete, is there any chance of fixing the broken engine?" James asked.

"No!" Pete answered. "It broke off and weighs 500 pounds."

James informed NASA of the predicament, and NASA called the President of the United States to tell him of the problem and see what could be done.

"Could Russia or China help us?" NASA asked the President.

He said, "I don't know, but I will check!"

The national news reported the situation to the country. Barbara Fox heard the news and went to find Mighty Mouse. She found Mighty Mouse and informed him that Sammy was marooned on the surface of Mars with Tommy and two astronauts. "Please help!" she exclaimed.

He said, "Here I go to save the day!" and took off to Mars.

When Mighty Mouse got to Mars, he found that everyone was okay. He loaded them into the landing capsule, flew it to the Space Shuttle Atlantis, put it in the shuttle bay, and closed the doors. He boosted the space shuttle on its way back to Earth and headed home. Mighty Mouse saved the day again! He is a hero!

The Space Shuttle Atlantis landed in California two weeks early. Mighty Mouse met the shuttle and flew Sammy and Tommy home. Their parents were glad to have their two little foxes home safe and sound but grounded them for one month for disobeying them! They had a great adventure that they told their friends and family about.

On Friday, a few days later, Bill came home excited after work and said, "The County Fair is in Chicago this weekend. Let's all go! We will catch the train tomorrow at 8:00 a.m. and be in Chicago by noon. We should be at the fairgrounds by 1:00 p.m. We can spend the night in the cattle barn. It will be great! What do you say?"

Sammy and Susan said, "Great!"

Barbara said, "It sounds like fun! I will make some sandwiches for the trip."

The next morning, they all got up and ran for the freight train. A few hours later, they were in Chicago. They had no trouble getting to the fairgrounds. They rode all the rides and ate their fill of popcorn and cotton candy.

A drunk man stepped on Susan's tail. Barbara bandaged it up, and then they went to watch the lumberjack race and chainsaw carving contest. After that, they went to bed. The next day they rode all the rides again before going home. The train was on time, and they made it home fine. They all had a good time!

The following Sunday, they all went to church. That day Pastor John taught them that Jesus Christ loved them and died and rose to pay our debt for our sins and that Jesus is God's only Son. At the end of the service, they went forward and got saved! They went home that day changed.

●　●　●

In another part of The Great Woods lived a family of black bears who were friends of the Foxes. The youngest bear was called Jack. His Dad, Mac, was a professional fisherman. He would catch, on average, about 25 salmon a day. He would leave five fish at home for the family and take the rest of the catch to the market and sell them. The mother bear was named June, and she maintained the cave and cared for her cub, Jack.

One day, Mac took Jack with him to work. He taught his fishing techniques to Jack. Mac got busy fishing and didn't notice that Jack was playing with his ball close to the banks of the raging river. Jack wasn't watching where he was and slipped, falling into the raging water.

"HELP!" he cried out. But unfortunately, Mac was too far away to save Jack when who should appear but Mighty Mouse.

"Here I come to save the day!" he said. Mighty Mouse swooped in, grabbed Jack by the back of his neck, and pulled him to safety. Mac was relieved and invited Mighty Mouse to dinner. They had a Bar-B-Q of salmon, baked beans, biscuits with honey, and Pepsi-Cola with ice cream for dessert. The food was good, and they all had a great time.

For the creatures of The Great Woods, life is good! And with God's help, they lived happily ever after!

THE END

THE DEADLY TAIL

Once upon a time, inside The Great Woods, there was a trail called The Blood Trail, which the inhabitants of the woods avoided. Many animals have died along this path at the hands of hunters, cougars, bears, dragons, and so on. It is rumored that hunters would hide out by the trail, stalking their prey. At night, a wise old owl, who lives near the path, warns the young and old creatures to be aware of the dangers that lurk along the trail and to be cautious about whom they befriend, because some animals will betray friends when it suits them.

In The Great Woods was a treacherous skunk named Bruce, who had an awful stink you could smell for miles. Bruce only had one friend: a bear named Tim. Tim could not smell Bruce's stench. However, Tim had a knack for tracking down beehives and honey. Tim's cave was at the edge of The Great Woods next to The Blood Trail. There were many orchards in Millersville at the east end of The Great Woods. Tim and Bruce loved eating apples. In the fall, they stored apples in Tim's cave.

The skunk told his bear friend, "Let's have a Bar-B-Q."

"Sounds great! What shall we have?"

The skunk replied, "Beef."

"Okay, I will start planning the menu and the guest list."

Every morning at 6:00 a.m., Tim would go fishing. After three or four hours of fishing, Tim would return to his cave for a nap. At sunset, he would rise and go hunting. He wanted to kill something because he was hungry. Bruce would go with him. Tim was a mean creature, and Bruce was sneaky. They would occasionally eat blueberries for dinner (they both loved them).

Bruce had devised a plan to trick a cow from a nearby farm into coming to The Blood Trail, and Tim would kill him. Bruce was known as a big, fat liar. Nevertheless, he told his plan to Tim, and they decided to execute it the next day at sunset.

The next day, Bruce snuck onto Farmers Brown's ranch and approached several of the cattle and said that a bundle of hay had fallen off a truck by the edge of The Great Woods and that he was having a party that evening, and they were all invited. He also was serving a salt block and plenty of fresh, clear spring water. The party would start at sunset. Several cows said they would be there. The trap was set.

At sunset, Bruce and Tim went back to the ranch. They found only one cow that was out in the open. Bruce enticed Bossy, the cow, to go with him. He led the cow to Tim's cave, where Tim was waiting. When they got there, Tim jumped Bossy and slit her throat. The cow was dead within minutes. Bruce and Tim prepared the meat for the Bar-B-Q.

Tim got his party invitations delivered to his friends and set up a bear jamboree.

The following day, Tim fired up the Bar-B-Q and started cooking. That night the party was on. They had carrots, green salad, hamburgers, steaks, honey, salt block, and spring water. After Bruce left, the bears struck up the band. (The other bears couldn't stand Bruce's smell.) The band comprised a bear on the jug, one on the banjo, one on an old broken guitar, and one on the harmonica. Animals heard the music and came from all around to enjoy the concert. When the show was over, Tim invited the animals from the audience to enjoy the leftovers from the party. That night was fun!

The following day, Tim went out fishing as usual. Bruce went and met him, and they went to lunch together and enjoyed blueberries. They talked about the duck hunting season scheduled for the following week.

A week later, the duck hunters arrived and set up their duck blinds, where they hid and waited for the ducks to fly by. A couple of hours later, a flock of mallards flew over, and Bang, Bang, Bang! The hunters had shot three ducks. The noise woke up Tim. He hated men. He came running from his cave, killed one hunter, and mauled two others. One of the injured hunters called for help on his cell phone. The paramedics came and transported them to the hospital.

They reported the incident to the sheriff. He dashed right out to the forest to check it out. He was looking around, and Tim jumped and mauled him. A short time later the deputy Sheriff was following up on the report, found the injured sheriff and took him to the hospital.

The deputy sheriff rounded up a posse to go after Tim. Finally, they reached The Great Woods and started the hunt. Hours later, they ran across Bruce.

One of the men said, "Shoot him. I hate skunks!"

Bruce said, "No! No! Don't shoot!" I heard you were looking for a mean black bear. I can give him to you!"

"Okay, where is he?" they asked.

Bruce replied, "The other side of The Great Woods near the Millersville entrance."

The posse followed Bruce over to Tim's cave. Bruce told them, "Wait here! I'll go get him!"

Bruce entered the cave and told Tim, "I brought a sheep over for you to feast on! It is waiting outside the cave. I will wait for you here. You know I hate all the blood of the kill!"

"Okay," Tim replied.

Tim left the cave and **BANG! BANG!** The posse shot him dead. Then, they said, "Let's cut off his head, mount it on a plaque, and hang it on the wall of the General Store so everyone knows we got him!" And that is what they did.

The Wise Old Owl was right: Be careful when choosing your friends: They should have good character and be loyal to you. That's what makes a good friend.

POETRY

A NEW YEAR TO REMEMBER

Happy New Year is what we say;
So Eat, Drink, and be Merry!
Our Debts and Problems are still here,
But on to the Next Year we go.
We flow our hopes and dreams into the New Year.
The fears and tears of life go with us and so we make a fuss!
And at Midnight, "Happy New Year" is heard everywhere!
New Resolutions abound to make us better.
Have Fun and Play for life is here;
As we try to steer our fate.
Easy does it! As the Holidays come to a close.
Enjoy the Sun and have some fun;
Have a Steak;
And make it a good year!
Joy is High and Hope is clear.
Remember to call on God;
As the Ball drops to start the New Year.
For God is on our side!
And God Bless America!

VALENTINES

Roses are Red—Violets are Blue; If you hate Valentine's
    Day then you are in the Stew!
As Cupid flew to heights unknown;
The dew of LOVE is in the air.
Which causes Believers to stare;
And friends to care.
As we buy flowers and candy to be fair to our loved ones;
And we look forward to days in the Sun.
Winter is ending and Summer is coming,
Just as fishing and swimming will soon be here.
So don't let anyone steer you wrong;
Let the songs of cheer dispel the Fear!
For God is on the scene.
Cards abound for fun and endless delight.
So take courage your date awaits!

ST. PATRICK'S DAY MAGIC

With St. Patrick's Day we count on the Irish for Luck;
As we look for the Pot of Gold at the end of the
    Rainbow!
The Leprechaun uses his lot to confound the lucky!
The magic of the day is kept in play by the four-leaf clover.
On this special day the Kiss of the Irish can bring luck!
And the rest of us wish to stay in the hay.
The Shamrock Shake makes the day complete.
Don't forget GREEN is in! Just like the Hills of Dover;
And the fields of Clover.
It is the Blarney Stone the Irish crave;
With Irish Coffee along the way.
St. Patrick's Day is here to stay!

AN EASTER WISH

One Beautiful Sunday—a long time ago—Our Savior,
    Lord, and King, Jesus Christ, arose from the grave!
In spite of the Cadbury, Peeps, Eggs, and Chocolate
    Bunnies everywhere.
We celebrate this at Church where Joy and Peace flow
    forth.
Easter Baskets abound to the glee of children everywhere.
On this day only joggers flee.
As we play searching for eggs with our family, the
    Winds blow:
To remind us to stay in God's Will.
The Daytona 500 will end the day.
With this hope we wish you a HAPPY EASTER and
    many more to come!

A GLORIOUS MOTHER'S DAY

One Bright and Sunny Day in May, A little birdie told
    me it is Mother's Day;
So with flowers in hand—I mounted my steed and off
    to Mother's House I go.
Where I found Mom asleep on the porch swing.
She arose with a start which scared my heart;
As off to Dinner we flowed.
With Love in my heart—I presented my card and
    flowers;
And sang out—Happy Mother's Day!
To my surprise Mom said, "I want to play!"
So we flew off to DisneyWorld.
With Mickey Mouse, Minnie, and Donald Duck we
    take our stand.
And Strike up the Band!
DisneyWorld is where we want to stay.
Whether Big Thunder Railroad, Splash Mountain, or
    the Haunted Mansion—It's all about Fun!
And playing in the Sun;
Because of the plan, we had a Glorious Time!
HAVE A HAPPY MOTHER'S DAY!

MOTHER'S DAY JOY!

It's Mother's Day so let's play;
When in Bed you want to stay.
As a Child you were always there for me; whether Soccer
    games or School Concerts.
You never neglected your job either.
Thank You Mom for all you do!
Your LOVE for us kept us going!
You always inspire us and give us hope.
HAPPY MOTHER'S DAY MOM!

FATHER'S DAY FUN

Father's Day is here;
There is no fear!
Whether a Golf Club or Tie the perfect gift is always near!
Cake and Baseball make a great match.
When in a Family they need a patch;
God is there to make the Catch.
Bar-B-Q's show our LOVE;
As Dad hears from above.
From NASCAR to Golf, Dad owns the day—Just as he
    wants it to be!
And at the picnic we want to stay;
But to the Car Show we go to play.
When our cars die Dad is there—To get us up in a flash.
Off to Church we go—
As God is in our flow.
When all is said and done;
There Dad is in the Sun!

THE TIME OF YEAR

From here to Eternity we do go—floating our Dreams
with us.
On this Fourth of July we make no fuss;
Because we know everything is in God's Hands.
The future is not ours to see, upon which we take a stand.
For freedom's Sake we do cope;
It is in God we find our Hope!
It is the scope of every American to celebrate Freedom
throughout the Land.
And we do boast about the Fireworks Shows.
Our Bar-B-Q's can be a bust, if only in God we put our Trust.
America flies high on the wings of eagles,
As our Fireworks display our Glee;
With honor and trust we flee.
Our Money says it best, "In God We Trust."
People of God rejoice;
And sing his praises.
Keep in mind the Rapture is at hand;
Where only God's best will stand!
At this Time of Year—Take Heart;
For those left behind will FART!
To the Marriage Supper of the Lamb only the faithful
will go.

HALLOWEEN EXCITEMENT

When the Pumpkins arise and Black Cats howl;
As Screams are heard from the Haunted Mansion in
Disneyland to Martha's Vineyard, "Trick or Treat."
You know Halloween has arrived!
Do you have enough candy?
As Bats take flight and Witches mix their brew;
Only the Owls stew over their fate;
As they are in Witch's Stew!
You must watch out for Skeletons on the prowl and
Hitchhiking Ghosts.
As Christians spend their time in Church exercising
their feat of Prayer.
After all the Fairs are done only Christmas adds
more fun!
With glee when all is done, we rest and enjoy the Noon
Day Sun.
We hope you had a glorious Halloween!

THE HOLIDAYS ABOUND

From here throughout Space—Thanksgiving has arrived.
Some people have trouble facing it;
Whether it's the cooking or the Parade—it makes basket
    cases of us all!
As we think of the Pilgrims and the Indians who made
    this Holiday so fair;
We Thank God for his Kindness and Love.
After which we get stuffed on Turkey and yams.
With Football running amuck, the fans run out shopping;
For Christmas is almost at hand.
The Salvation Army has taken their stand.
With bells a ringing and carolers singing,
Peace on Earth—Good Will to Men.
Strike up the Band to Celebrate—The Holidays are at hand.
We share our Joy with friends at Starbucks.
From there with care we set up the Christmas Tree.
Where Presents abound for you and me.
In the middle of it all, Santa does his thing.
As Christmas ends we look forward to a New Year.
Just think in twelve months—it starts all over again!

CHRISTMAS AT HEART

HO . . . HO . . . HO and Hallelujah! Jesus Christ is born!
From St. Nicholas to Jesus Christ people are torn.
Which is fiction and which is truth?
As a stitch in time—Tradition fails us!
God's Son came to Earth so long ago;
To Save Man from Sin and Hell,
Thanks to his Death and Resurrection!
Hanukkah arrives to celebrate lights.
One Thing is clear—Christmas is here!
So with nothing to fear we light our Christmas Trees.
Presents abound to the glee of little ones.
So have some fun baking cookies in the Sun.
Since God is near—off to Church we go;
Singing, "Oh Come Let Us Adore Him."
So Santa does his thing to make Hearts merry.
As we host friends on Christmas Day—We terry and
    are Thankful.
While on the Coast Surfers play;
We at home want to stay.
Christmas comes but once a year so enjoy the fun and
    Pray for Peace on Earth—Good Will to Men!

OUR MODERN CHRISTMAS

HO . . . HO . . . HO! And Merry Christmas!
When Jesus throws a Birthday party, It is a Great Affair!
NO ONE who knows him is left out and everyone
  wants to stare.
From the Grinch to St. Nicholas, all are invited—
  including the pairs.
And if you think this Party is Great,
Just wait till you see his State Wedding and the
  Wedding Supper of the Lamb for his Bride (the
  Church).
And the guests that will be there—What a fate!
You can be there too if you make JESUS CHRIST your
  Savior and Lord (as part of the Church).

THE BIRTHDAY EXPERIENCE

It's your Birthday and now you are a year older;
And at this stage of Life—it's time to travel.
You are now Officially Old!
Never fear for God is near.
Look up and cheer for your redemption draweth nigh.
Remember you only turn this old once!
So when you gas up your car to take a trip;
Eat, Drink and reminisce for life is short;
As off to DisneyWorld we go.
Whether riding Space Mountain or Pirates of the
    Caribbean;
Our mission is clear; to grab some gusto whenever it
    appears!
It truly is a Small, Small World!
Enjoy Life to the fullest!
And Happy Birthday and we wish you many more!

A BIRTHDAY TO REMEMBER

With Cake and Balloons the Party goes;
And another year older the Birthday flows.
So Happy Birthday we sing and away we go into
    another year.
There is no need to fear for God is here!
Dinners and Movies we enjoy with glee;
Work and chores we flee.
To view the Sports Scene we agree;
Is a haven for our Special Day,
Where all we want to do is play;
And Home is where we want to stay!
Flowers are nice but work prevails for its Money is
    needed to provide the frills.
Though Life goes on—Enjoy the Thrills!
HAPPY BIRTHDAY to our Special Person
With many more on the Horizon!

FLORIDA ADVENTURE

From here to DisneyWorld we go;
So our Hearts to Florida do flow.
As Carried on the Wings of Delta we do fly;
As Carried through the Sky like on Eagles Wings.
To the glory of the great rides of the Magic Kingdom—
    With Fireworks galore!
From King Kong to Jaws the thrills do go;
To discover Universal Studios is in our flow.
As the Souvenirs we do score.
At Cape Kennedy the rockets soar!
Peace and Joy we want to find;
When at the restaurants we go and dine.
With Disney—MGM Studios we go to War—Star
    Wars that is!
Once the Galaxy is safe, we return home to rejoin the
    work of God.

GLORIOUS HAWAII

Aloha and Welcome greets visitors as they arrive in Paradise.
From the shores of Waikiki Beach to the Fern Grotto—
    Paradise awaits!
We thrive at the Sights of the Islands.
Hawaii truly is Paradise; the Jewel of the Pacific.
Hula Dancers adorn the Hawaiian Cultural Center.
With Swimming, Golf, and Luaus we find the Islands
    glorious and there we hang loose.
Blow Holes and Black Sand Beaches are a typical kind
    of thing for Hawaii.
The signs of Agriculture show up as Coffee,
    Macadamia Nuts, and Pineapple.
Waimea Canyon is where beauty and Creation meet;
This is where God's handiwork is displayed.
We are humbled at the Arizona Memorial where our
    Patriotism survives!
Your trip to Hawaii is not complete without a visit to
    the Iolani Palace;
The only Royal Residence in the United States.

NEVADA FURY

Racing whether horse or car is a rush;
Which gives gamblers a blush!
With the CLANG, CLANG, CLANG of Slot
    Machines tells you we are in Nevada.
And Las Vegas is plush and full of games to the dealer's
    delight;
As losers take flight.
Cards abound with Hearts and Jacks;
And Kings bring Aces home to roust.
And in the distance a rare winner is heard.
From Dice to Bingo—Reno awaits.
So with tickets in hand—the Stage Shows prepare.
From the Stratosphere to the MGM GRAND—
    Nevada displays its flair!
The Casinos endure as hope flourishes in the air.
As the winners care.
With dice in hand we take our stand for Freedom!

COFFEE YOUR DAY

Coffee and Donuts make the World go around.
So Party Hardy!
The day will flow no matter where you go;
Stow your problems as off to work we go!
And they say, "No Coffee—No Talkie."
So get your Cup of Jo and off to work we go!
As the Coffee Shop Employees perk.
Jerks come and go, but the regulars endure.
So tow your Bod to the Coffee and the Donuts will
    follow!

GET WELL!

As we age, Pain becomes part of Life;
Stress and Strife are also part of Life.
When in the Hospital you do go;
Remember to Hang In There! And get well!
Just as the bang of the drum signals the Band's arrival
    in the parade;
Doctors and Nurses do their thing to bring you back to Life.
Try not to let pain stain your life.
So hurry up and get well because you are Needed!

THE UNFAITHFUL FRIEND

When stabbed in the back by a friend—What do you do?
When trust is gone can you believe?
Or what will you achieve without him or her?
When tears and fears arrive—You Must Stand!
For God is at hand.
It hurts a lot—but God is on the spot!
So flirt with your girl or guy and hang on tight;
For Joy comes in the morning!
Use this ploy at work to achieve success!
And remember God is the Best Friend you can ever
    have—He never fails!
At Christmas we celebrate Jesus Christ's Birth;
Just as kids sat on Santa's knee, we Believe!
Do we whack or beat the heck out of them?
We want to attack them for what they have done;
It is better to forget them and have some Fun!
Baking cookies in the Sun.
When all is said and done, God is the only one we have
    to please!
So don't waste your time on them;
Remember when they tease;
It is you they have to please!

THANK YOU

With a Joyful Heart I say Thank You!
You have always been there for me.
On you we depend!
I enjoy the privilege of _____.
Your Humor and Personality are contagious;
We spend our time on joyous work;
At this our attention perks.
Your kindness is legendary!
So to our good friend we say, "THANK YOU!"
And have a great day!

HAPPY TRAILS

From here to Eternity you will go;
Taking our Gratitude with you for a job well done!
As you go to your next position remember the fun you
    had here.
When you lay out in the Sun your future at hand;
Don't stick your head in the sand.
There is no need to fear for God is near;
So stay in the center of God's Will!
And fill your Life with joy.
Make your strife count as your days go by;
Always reach for the sky!
Now as we part ways—we wish you HAPPY TRAILS!

THE LEGEND OF DEAD-EYE HARVEY

One day in May, Dead-Eye Harvey got a call . . .
HELP! My house's skin is peeling!
So off to the customer; Dead-Eye flew on his white
    steed Thunder.
The client's house was about to fall.
Dead-Eye climbed off his steed with paint gun in hand.
He took his stand and fired—A Giant Cloud filled
    the air.
There was no need to care—For Dead-Eye was there!
When the cloud parted what should appear, but a
    Brilliant Castle . . . Freshly Painted of Course!
The customer proclaimed—"YOU SAVED
    THE DAY!"
"Now it's time to play!"
And Dead-Eye Exclaimed as he rode out of sight . . . It's
    easy as Pie;
Just call Dead-Eye!
And that my friends is the legend of Dead-Eye Harvey.

JOHN WAYNE—AN AMERICAN HERO

When we think of the West and its history;
Only one name comes to mind—Big John …Wayne
    that is!
He was best with his guns and great with his fists.
The Duke was tall in the saddle among the setting Sun.
This American Hero has been seen having Fun fighting
    in all our Wars on the Silver Screen.
Big John was Six Foot Two with eyes of Blue;
His kindness landed him in the stew at times.
To Children he flew to the heights of Eagles;
It was his antics women adored!
When he was sick he turned to our Lord Jesus Christ
    for Salvation.
And now with the Angels he soars!
The Duke taught Boys how to be Men!
If he were here today—he would say: I drank too much
    and got into too many fights.
And I should have spent more time in the Church's
    Light and God's Sight!

CLASSIC ANTIQUE CARS

The Best of the Antique Cars is by far the Packard!
It is not made anymore, but boy what a Car!
Only a Star shines as bright as a Classic Car!
Cadillac and Lincoln are far out!
They make us want to fly.
Rolls Royce and Mercedes Benz set the bar high.
Everywhere muscle cars abound;
These are the Toys Men love!
Pontiac gave us chills with the GTO and Trans Am.
Today the Chevy Corvette is King of the Hill—and we
    make a great fuss!
We can't forget FORD gave us the Thunderbird and
    Mustang.
The Auto Show reveals the best that has ever been.
And the racetrack demonstrates the power of these
    machines.
From the Grand Prix to Indy they go.
With sales to the Sky—Volkswagen flowed.
To Car Lovers everywhere—we say Thank You!
See you at the Car Shows!

THE SUPPLY TRUCK

To Truck or NOT to Truck that is the Challenge;
Whether we have the Time and Fortitude to defeat the
    Giant; like David against the Goliath of Old!
Gives pause to refresh ourselves!
Can we conquer this Beast with our Box-Cutters and
    Water-Bottles is yet to be seen;
Henceforth we attack to the cheers of our Coaches!
As fears assail we slice those boxes and process those
    clothes;
And Cookware flows.
The race is afoot;
As we go forth and Conquer!
We live to fight another day!

LOVE GOES AROUND

The LOVE of a Beautiful Woman is amazing to
    behold;
And that of a Faithful man is Pure Gold.
It is said that Love makes the World go around, but
    does it?
It's Love and Kindness that is worthy to behold!
LOVE is the cause of Marriage, Divorce, and Children;
Or so it is believed.
So is Marriage the Goal to be achieved?
God gave us the first couple and the first marriage.
There is a common saying: "WHAT DOES LOVE
    HAVE TO DO WITH IT?"
So don't have a fit—LOVE the feeling.
Because a breakup leaves a hole in the Heart that is
    hard to heal.
Only time can help the feel;
To build a family is a fine deal.
Listening or not to your mate can seal your fate!
So only LOVE can find a way!

A TASK WELL DONE

The Flowers of Spring make the Birds sing.
Work is the fling of Life.
The exercise it provides adds spice to life;
At what price do we enjoy leisure and rest.
Our Strength and Energy we apply to the task;
With our paycheck in hand as our reward for a job
    well done!
After which we go have some Fun;
So we enjoy picnics in the Sun.
At work laziness doesn't fit;
As management agrees!
Hard work is key as we see bees spin honey for the Queen;
We press on to Success as we aid our customers with
    their needs!

FACING DEATH

From here to Eternity with hope we go;
Through Jesus Christ our Lord and Savior.
When Death touches our family,
We experience loss and grief; Empathy and Sympathy
    of friends.
When we face Death our family matters most;
Whether here or Coast to Coast.
The scope of Heaven or Hell gives us pause;
Our Life is the cause.
We rely on hope from the Holy Bible and God above;
If we know our Heavenly Father or not matters!
The Glory of Heaven is here for the Believer.
All others have Fear and Dread!
So when the tear comes—Put your Faith in Jesus Christ;
He is the author and finisher of our faith and hope!

THE RETAIL CHALLENGE

To Tag or Not to Tag—That is the Question?
Whether it is nobler to endure the slings and arrows of
      outrageous fortune;
Or embrace _____ Store Name _____ policies—gives us
      pause . . . to reminisce.
To Sell or Not to Sell can be an Issue;
Whether Furniture or Clothes,_____ Store Name _____
      can't be beat!
As we march into the Holidays; Santa sings: "Jingle Bells."
The customer tells us, "GOOD JOB!"
_____ Store Name _____ bets on us and we win.
We go from Truck to Truck with tissue in hand;
Only the righteous will stand.
To Bail or NOT to Bail . . . Cardboard . . . is not the
      question . . . It's Reality.
To Sleep and yet to Dream;
To Hope knowing God is on our side.
To Be or NOT to Be—We look to him.
From here to Eternity we do go;
With Movies, Fairs, and Rodeos on hand.
Only the Faithful will stand;
So strike up the Band for _____ Store Name _____!

DIABETES—THE SHAMEFUL KILLER

As Day sparks to Life;
The Meadowlarks begin tossing.
We are all reminded another day has dawned.
To those with Diabetes the strife and pain endure.
The disease that kills so many Americans;
It takes the frills of life away!
We can't forget the strife and courage it takes to live
    with this disease.
Our Hope comes from God—the author and finisher
    of our faith;
He alone can heal us of our disease!
With Fear and Dread we face what other diseases
    Diabetes will bring upon us.
We feel pain whether amputation or Death;
Diabetes steals joy from Life!
So when tears come—family matters most!
As we try to restore joy back into our lives;
At what point will the Grim Reaper show?
Follow the Sugar Trail and you will know.
Don't forget your fate is in your hands!

SUPER BOWL GLORY

From here to the Super Bowl we go;
One glorious Sunday in February.
With Coca-Cola, Chips, or Popcorn in hand;
We stow the good stuff for Half-Time.
As Kick-off comes we take our stand.
The Offense has their plan;
It's to the End-Zone we go.
The Defense does its best to make a stand;
But then it's SCORE—Touchdown!
The Fans Roar and it's the Extra Point.
Then back and forth it goes and the next we know it's
    Half-Time.
We can't forget the Music Spectacular at the Half!
In Today's game is it _____Team Name_____ or
    _____Team Name_____ that will overcome.
It's Football that makes today's action flow.
The pace is frantic;
Then the Final Gun—Who has Won?
The announcers scramble—it's Trophy Time!
And the Champion is Crowned.
What a Day!

THE DAY THE DONKEY DIED

President Trump endured;
As Freedom is Secured!
And Old Glory still flies.
Just as America tries to unite once again.
The economy is in a Great State;
But Democrats have seen their Fate!
After the Speaker of the House shot their Donkey with
her 308-millimeter Impeachment Rifle.
Some people say she had too much on her plate.
Now the Democrats have nothing to ride to the Winner's
Circle.
And there goes their pride because it is too far to walk.
Long live the Republic;
And God Bless America!

UNCLE SAM IS AT HAND

From Form 1040 to April 15th we go;
As taxes upon us flow!
We pay through the nose—to make our Government go.
Whether Taxation or War—Uncle Sam is there to
    inspire this nation.
He counts on God to protect it.
As to the November Election we go.
Republican or Democrat we prepare;
The Future will be a scare!
With President Trump we can compare;
For he has the flair!
From Taxes to the Election—The NEWS gives us
    little hope;
So to God we focus our scope which provides new hope!

THE BIBLE

The Bible is Life's Owner's Manual;
Through which God shows his Love, Righteousness,
   Grace, Mercy, and Justice to Mankind.
Starting in the Garden of Eden with the fall of man
      to the Tower of Babel to the Fiery Furnace to the
      White Throne Judgement—God is there and cares!
Don't Stifle the Holy Spirit!
It's the trifles that matter most;
Whether here or Coast to Coast—Jesus Christ is Lord!
Moses brought us the Law and Jesus Christ brought us
      Salvation!
We can't forget that the Rapture is upon us.
So we fuss and study our Bibles to be ready.
God warned Nineveh and America of possible disaster;
He wants his people to turn to him so he can heal
      our Land.
Be steady in your faith in Christ!
If in the Lion's Den or Prison you know God is Faithful!
Only Jesus can forgive shameful Sin.
Proclaim the news to your kin—Jesus is coming soon!
The Anti-Christ will appear and God will get his
      revenge.
As the Blood Moons attest—the Tribulation will break
      forth.
Heaven awaits the believers in Christ!

BIBLE PROPHECY

When the Bible talks about the End: ARE WE
    TELLING OUR FAMILY and FRIENDS?
The Russians are planning to attack Israel;
And God will kill 5/6 of them.
The Anti-Christ is spanning the Globe;
His Worship he will demand!
With his Mark (666)—the people he will probe.
To Eat or Not to Eat will be part of his plan.
With the Two Witnesses and the 144,000 God to the
    rescue!
To Die or Not to Die, Christians must take a stand!
Trust in Jesus Christ to make Heaven our Home;
A One World Government is on the Horizon.
In the Rapture we have our hope;
For the Future is within our scope.
Jesus Christ stops Armageddon;
As he Judges the Nations—He is Tops!
Jesus Christ will reign the Earth Forever!
Satan (The Devil) meets his End!

WHAT THE FUTURE HOLDS

To the Future we do go . . . whether alone or together;
With God—together we flow.
We give him Glory while we stow our past;
To DisneyWorld or Heaven we are called;
As we wait to see what God's Plan has for me and you!
We fan God's Love for us;
To the Holy Bible we take our stand.
For only God can lend a hand.
Our goals we give to him;
And he directs us to Score!
As the Kingdom awaits.

HOPE

In God we find our Hope;
For Jesus Christ is in our Scope.
When COVID-19 strikes;
And your Fever Spikes;
Only God can put out the flames!
Hope through Jesus Christ's Death and Resurrection;
And soon coming return.
As we float through Life;
To Be or Not To Be that is the Question asked by all!
What is NEXT and where do we go from here?
To the Bible we go and search.
We see God on his Perch—rewarding Believers and
    Wrath for the rest.
Glory to God—He is the Best!

HERE WE GO AGAIN

For Freedom and Uncle Sam,we strike up the Band;
With equality and unity, we take our stand!
On July Fourth the Fans of America Show their Pride;
And God is on our side.
We have Fireworks on the Day;
As we hang out and play.
To the Beach we want to go to Sun ourselves on
    the Sand.
The Surf relaxes the mind;
When Peace we want to find.
At the Olive Garden we go and dine.
The people of God come together in Love;
No matter their differences—That come from above.
Our hope is in God's Hands;
While we prepare for Heaven;

We go . . . Back . . . . . .
. . . . . . To The FUTURE!

A FOND FAREWELL

From here to the Future you will go;
With fond memories that will flow.
As with our gratitude for a job well done.
You will cherish your time in the Sun;
With your friends at hand in your new job you take a
    stand.
Enjoying time at the Beach with your feet in the sand.
As the years fly by always reach for the Sky;
And keep family close by.
Remember there is no need to fear for God is here!
If a tear should come—have faith and we will meet again;
Till then—HAPPY TRAILS!

ABOUT THE AUTHOR

I worked as a telephone man before I retired. During that time, I traveled a lot and got some great ideas for stories from my work and journeys. I started telling these stories to my friends and family. At family get-togethers, these stories have often been the highlight, and something we all look forward to.

I really hope you enjoy these stories too. My goal is just to share the fun and joy these tales have brought to my family and friends. Whether these stories make you laugh or just give you something to think about, I hope they add a little bit of fun to your day.

www.ingramcontent.com/pod-product-compliance
Lightning Source LLC
Chambersburg PA
CBHW060132260626
47160CB00005B/2074